I HATE SUPERMAN!

by Louise Simonson

Illustrated by Kevin and Kathy Altieri

Little, Brown and Company
Boston New York Toronto London

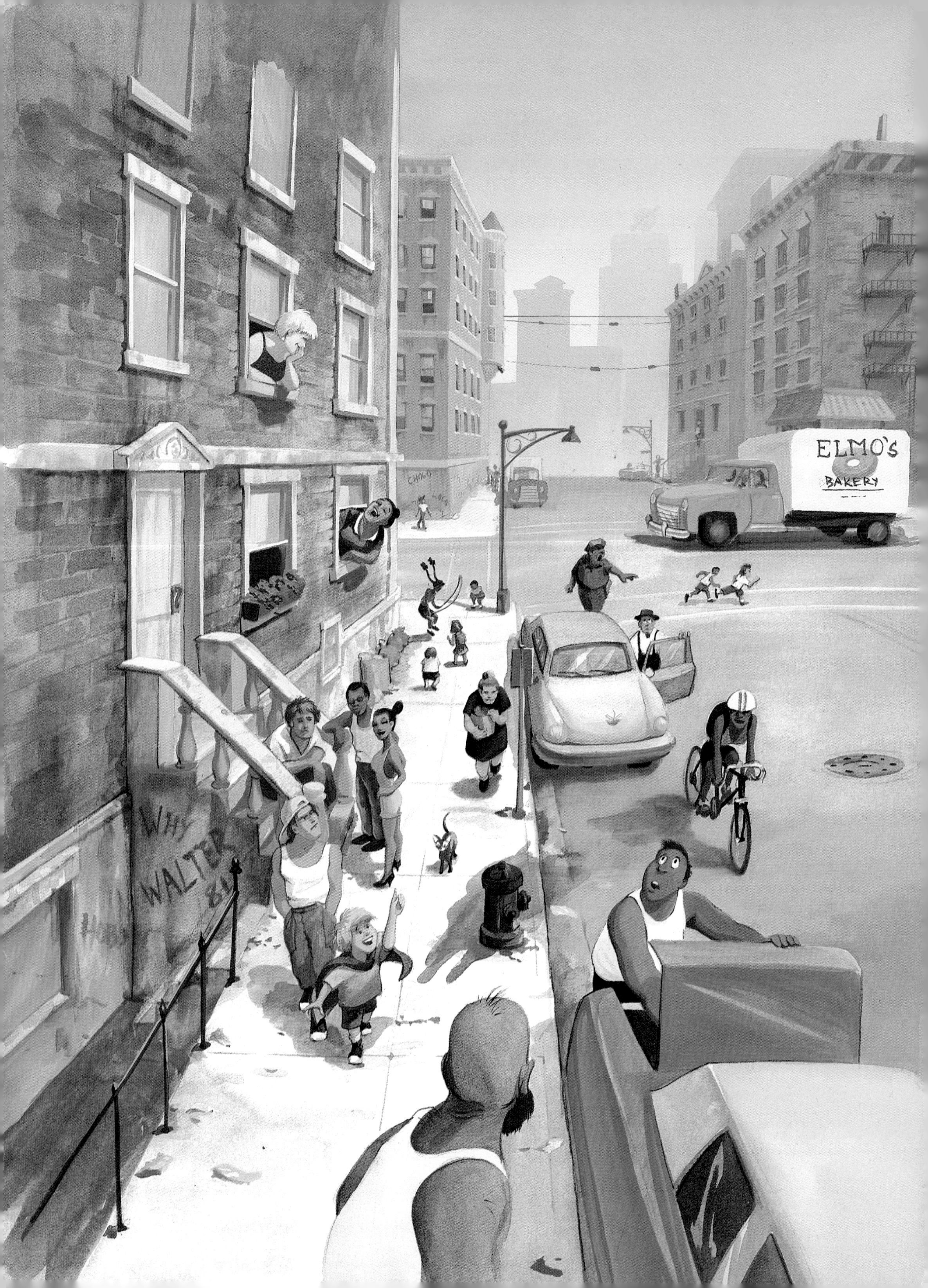
ELMO'S
BAKERY

"Our apartment is sweltering, but it's even hotter on the street!" James grumbled to his brother Mike.

"Maybe you should ditch the Superman cape," Mike suggested.

"No way!" James said. "Can't we go down to Mr. Masire's and get a soda instead?"

"Sure," Mike agreed. As they walked together down the block, James heard the snap of gunfire, like firecrackers on the Fourth of July. But he wasn't scared. The sound came from several blocks away, and he knew Mike would protect him.

His mother knew it, too. During the summer, she often left James with his brother while she went to work.

But there was another reason James ignored the gunfire. Superman!

Far up in the sky the Man of Steel was flying toward the trouble spot. James was sure that if *he* were ever in trouble, Superman would help him, too.

"Head straight home when you're finished!" Mike said. James went into the grocery store while Mike walked down to the corner to hang out with some new friends James didn't like very much. Something about them made him uncomfortable.

Every time James visited Mr. Masire, the old grocer would tell him about the time his car skidded off the road during a blizzard, and how Superman rescued him. "Now, there's a real hero," Mr. Masire always ended his story.

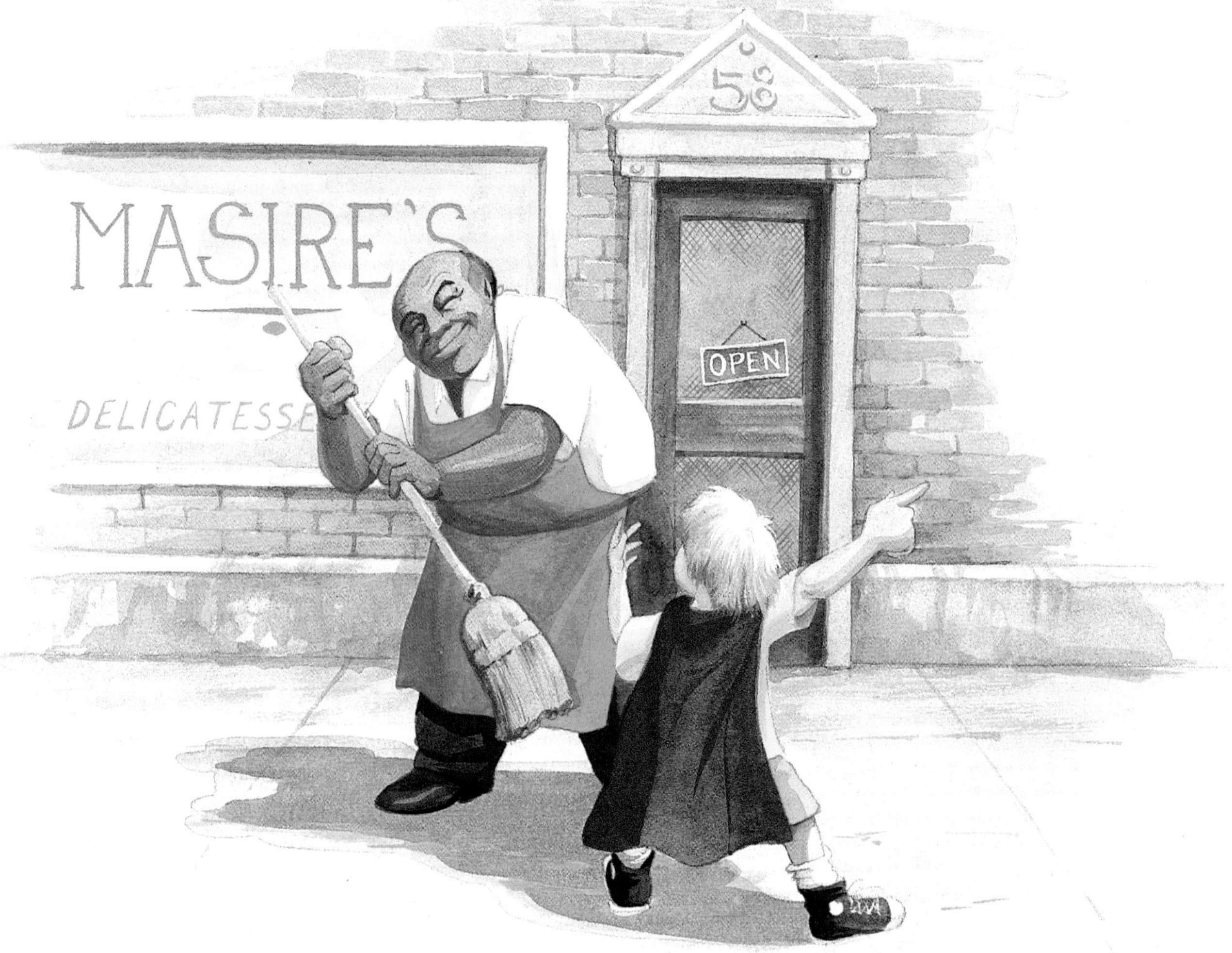
58
MASIRE'S
DELICATESSE
OPEN

James would nod and grin. And together they would search the skies for Superman.

As often as not, they spotted him flying overhead.

He was the guardian of the city of Metropolis. And he was James's hero.

James ran to the corner, eager to tell his brother that he and Mr. Masire had seen Superman again. His brother was standing in an alley with his wanna-be gangster friends, wrecking the neighborhood, spray-painting an ugly picture of Superman on the wall.

"No!" James shouted, running up to him. "Don't! He's my hero!"

Mike's friends looked at the red towel pinned around James's neck, and they laughed. "Look at him! The little punk thinks *he's* Superman!"

James looked at his brother. He was afraid that Mike would laugh at him, too. But, instead, he put his arm around James. "Leave him alone!" Mike said. "I used to think Superman was cool when I was little, too!"

James grinned up at his brother. At that moment he thought that Mike was even cooler than Superman.

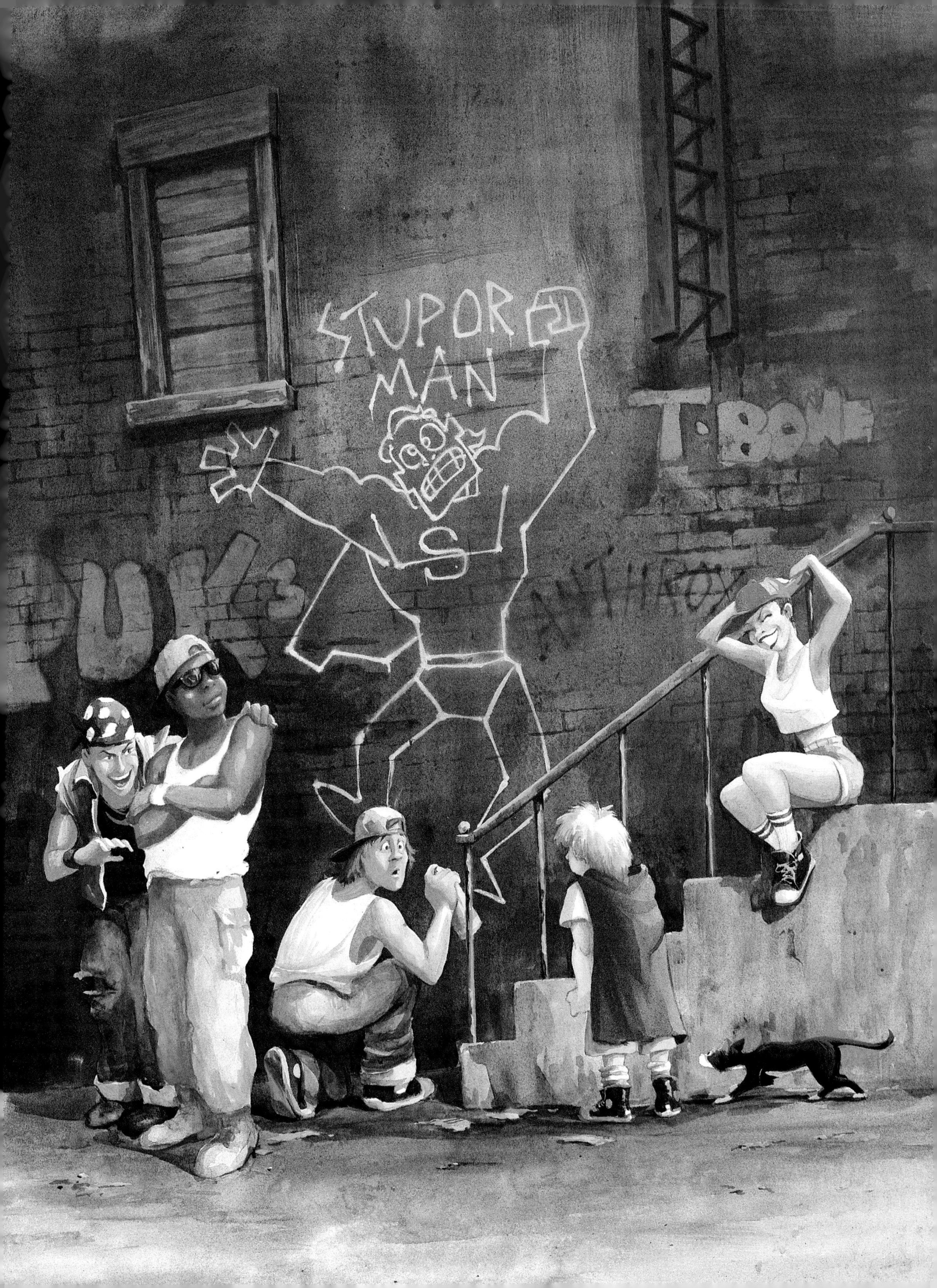
STUPOR MAN
S
T-BONE

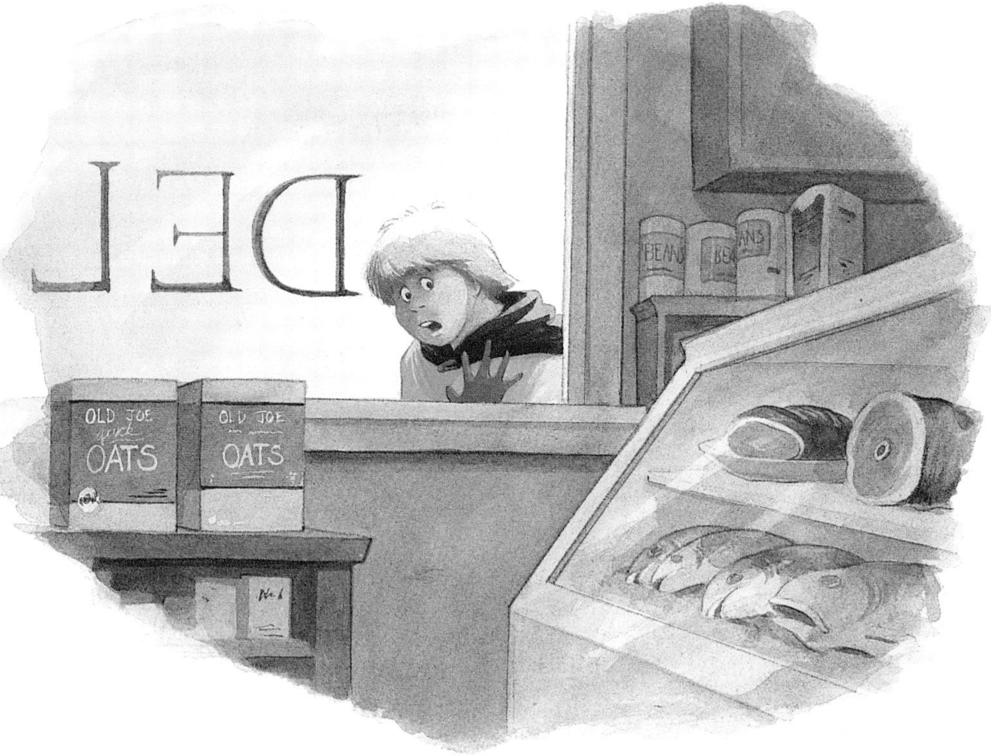
OLD JOE
OATS
OLD JOE
OATS

Several days later James ran down the street with quarters from the change jar jingling in his pocket. His mother had phoned Mike from work to ask him to buy milk, but Mike wasn't home. "What's with that boy lately?" she asked. "You run down to Mr. Masire's store for me, James, and pick up a quart. He's likely to close before I get home. I'll deal with Mike later," she added.

Mike's probably hanging out late with his new friends, James thought. His brother would catch it when he got home.

When James arrived at Mr. Masire's, the store windows were dark. *That's strange*, James thought. *Mr. Masire never closes his store before eight.* James cupped his hands around his eyes and peered through the glass. He saw shadowy figures inside.

It's a robbery! James thought quickly. *I've got to get help!*

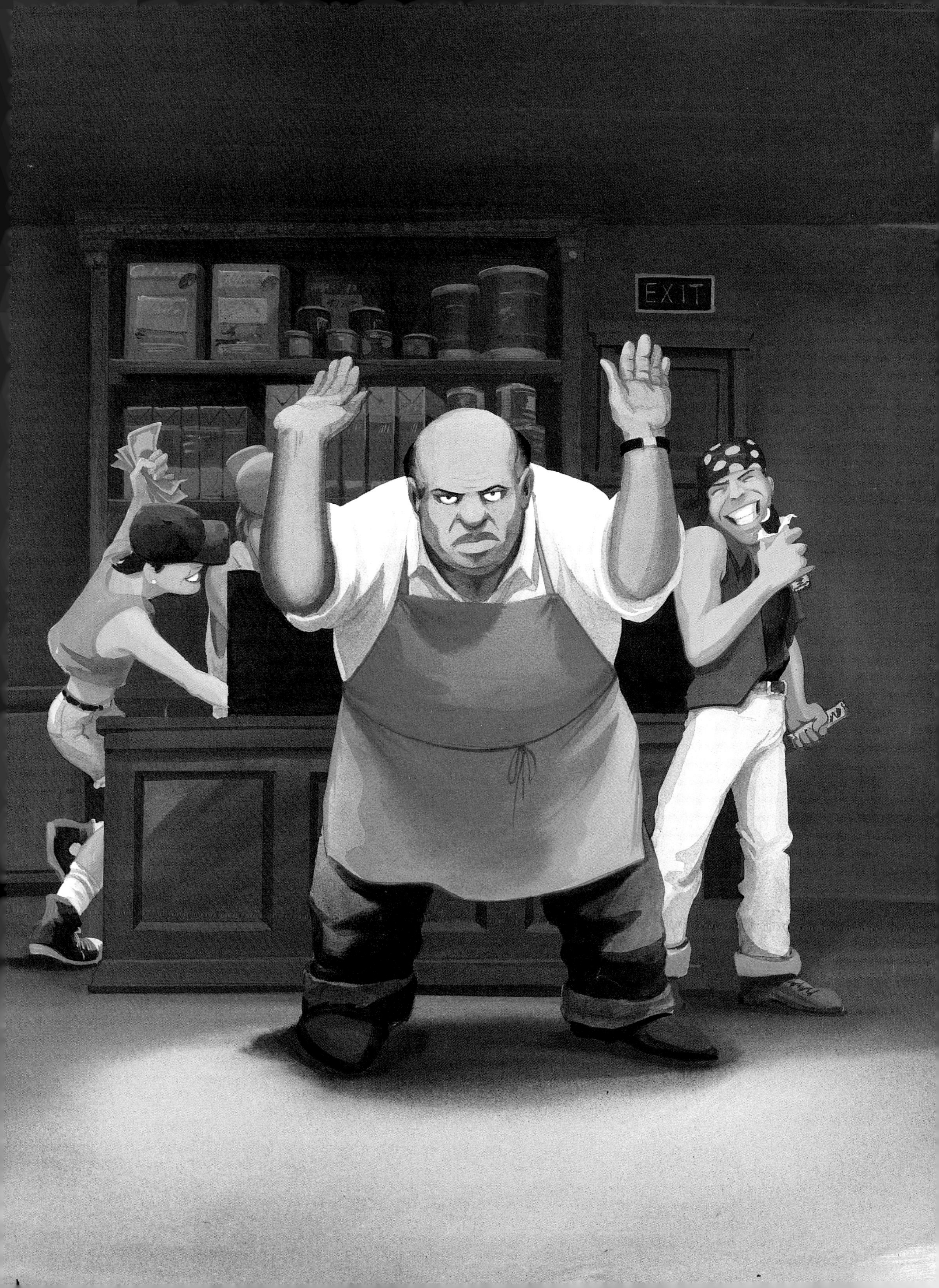
EXIT

Outside, a group of tough-looking gang members were the only people in sight. *They wouldn't help Mr. Masire,* James thought as he ran toward a phone booth. *The gangs are mad at him because he won't take sides in their fights. I'll call 911 and get the police!*

James snatched up the phone. That's when he saw Superman flying over the *Daily Planet* building. He suddenly remembered that Superman could hear anything, even from far away.

"Superman!" James yelled. "Somebody's robbing Mr. Masire's store! Please! You've got to help!"

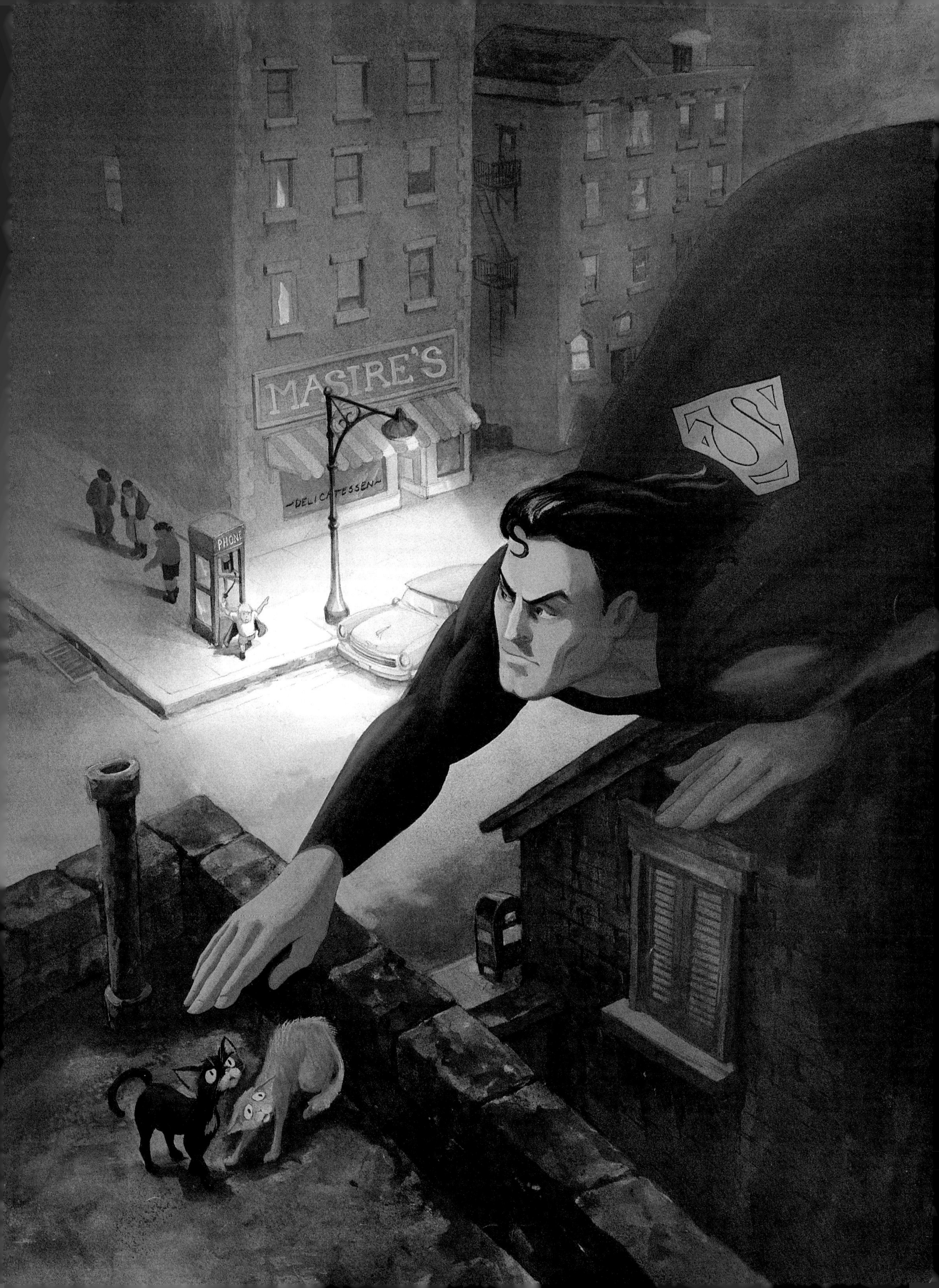
MASIRE'S
DELICATESSEN
PHONE

Superman looked toward Mr. Masire's store. "One of them has a gun!" he shouted down to James. "Stay away! This is dangerous!"

He knows there's a gun because he can see right through the wall, James thought with pride as he watched his hero dive and disappear into the store.

BAM! BAM! BAM! BAM! BAM!

James heard rapid gunfire, but he didn't run.

James knew all about Superman. How he came to Earth from another planet. How he could fly. How he was the strongest man in the world, and the fastest, too. He could do anything. Surely he would save Mr. Masire.

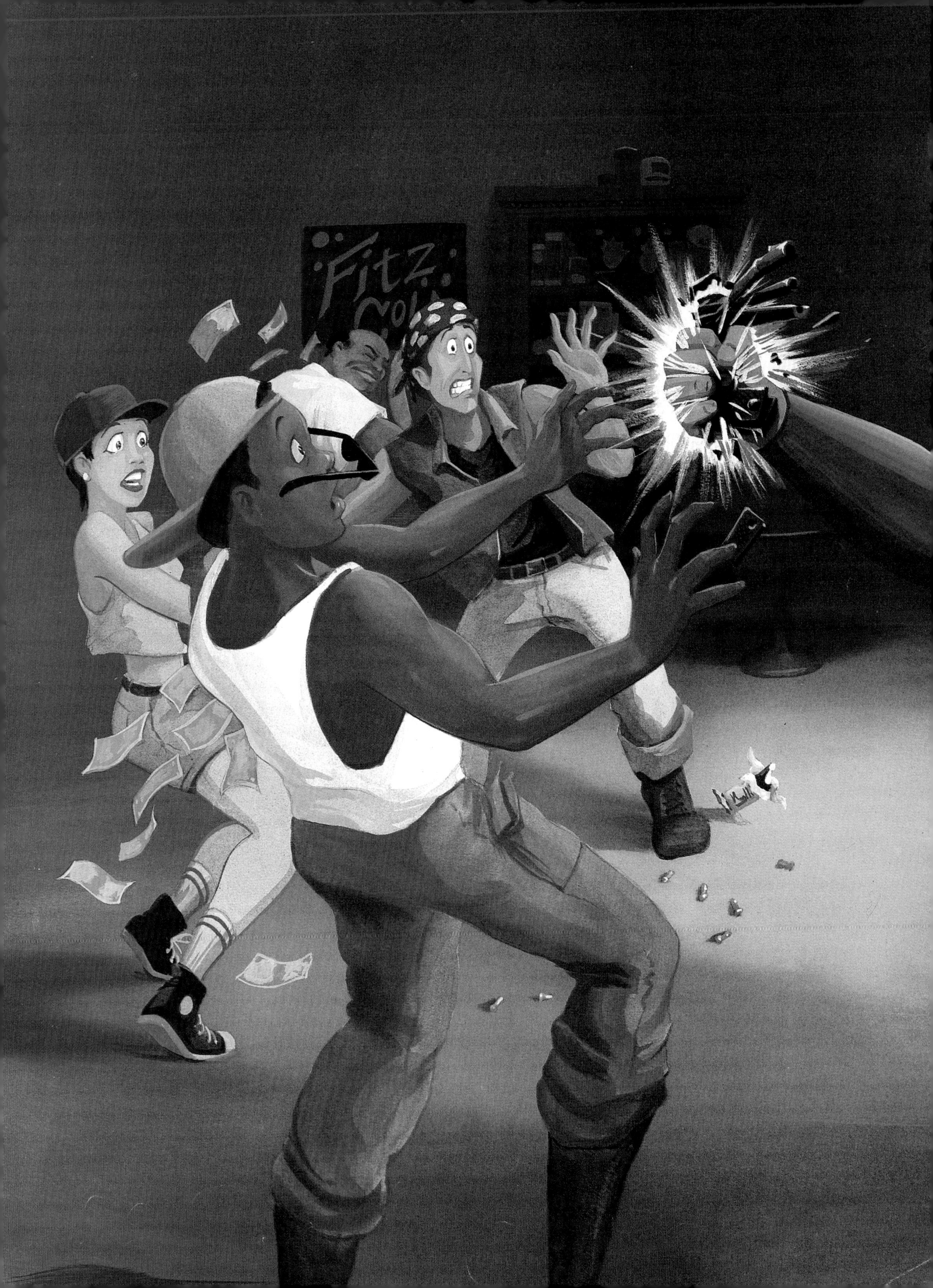
Fitz

When the gunfire stopped, James peered in the window. He could tell the fight was over, so he slipped inside the door. "You did it, Superman!" he cheered.

As the smoke from the gunfire cleared, James saw that Superman had caught the robbers. One of them was turned away, but James knew him anyway. His heart sank. "You can't take him, Superman!" James cried, running toward them. "It's a mistake. That's my brother!"

"I'm sorry," Superman said softly. "But I have to turn them all over to the police. Your brother wasn't the one with the gun, but he was breaking the law. Mr. Masire could have been wounded."

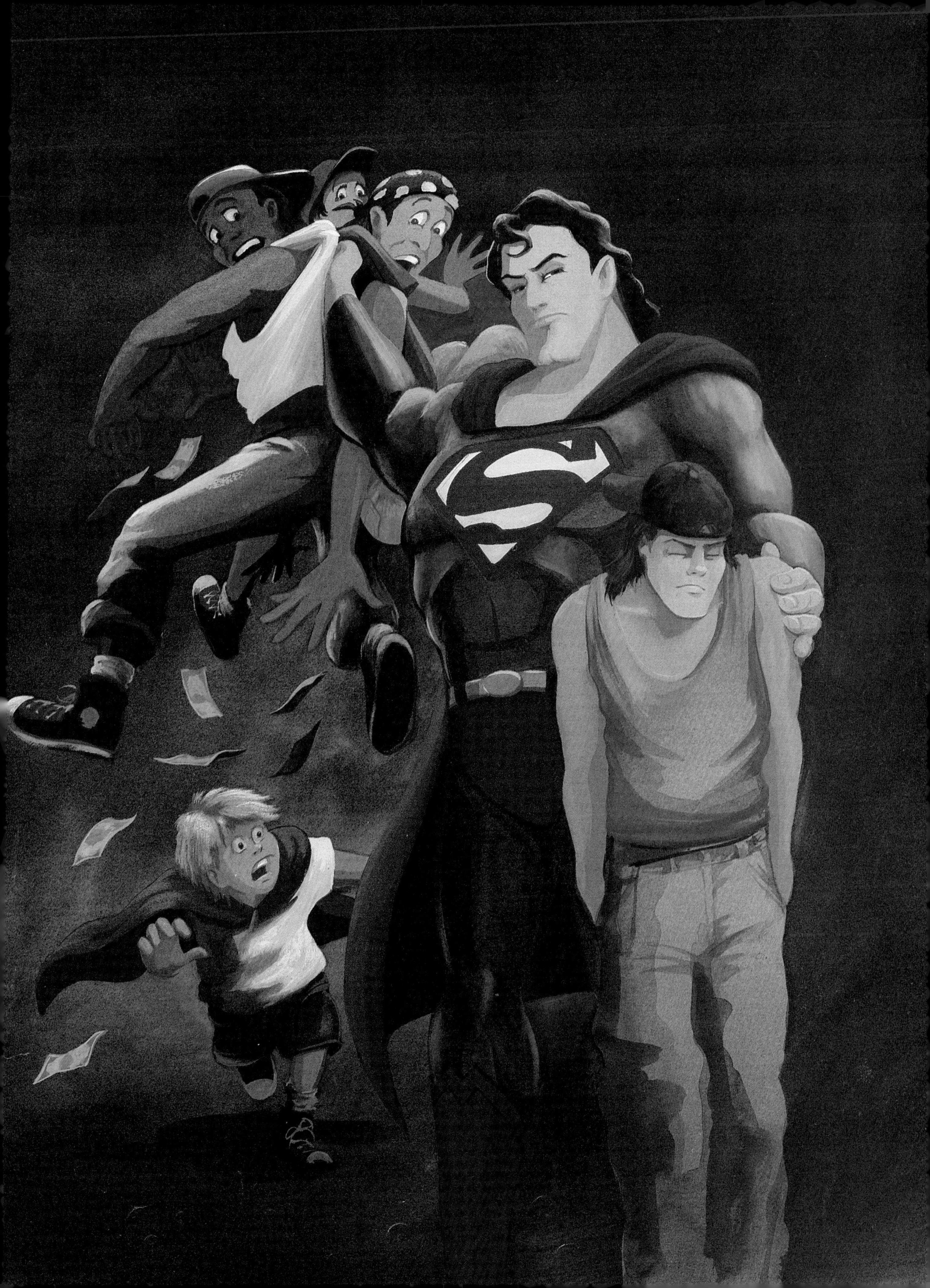

That night, James was still upset after he and his mother returned from the police station. He stormed into his room and slammed the door.

Mr. Masire thinks I'm a big hero. But Mom is crying. And Mike wouldn't even look at me! He hates me for snitching on him. Forcing back his tears, James ripped the Superman cape from around his neck and stuffed it in the trash.

He shouldn't have been robbing Mr. Masire. But Mike isn't a bad guy, James thought as he tore his favorite pictures of Superman off the wall. *Superman should have let him go!*

Then James saw the can of Day-Glo spray paint on top of his brother's dresser. And he knew what he had to do.

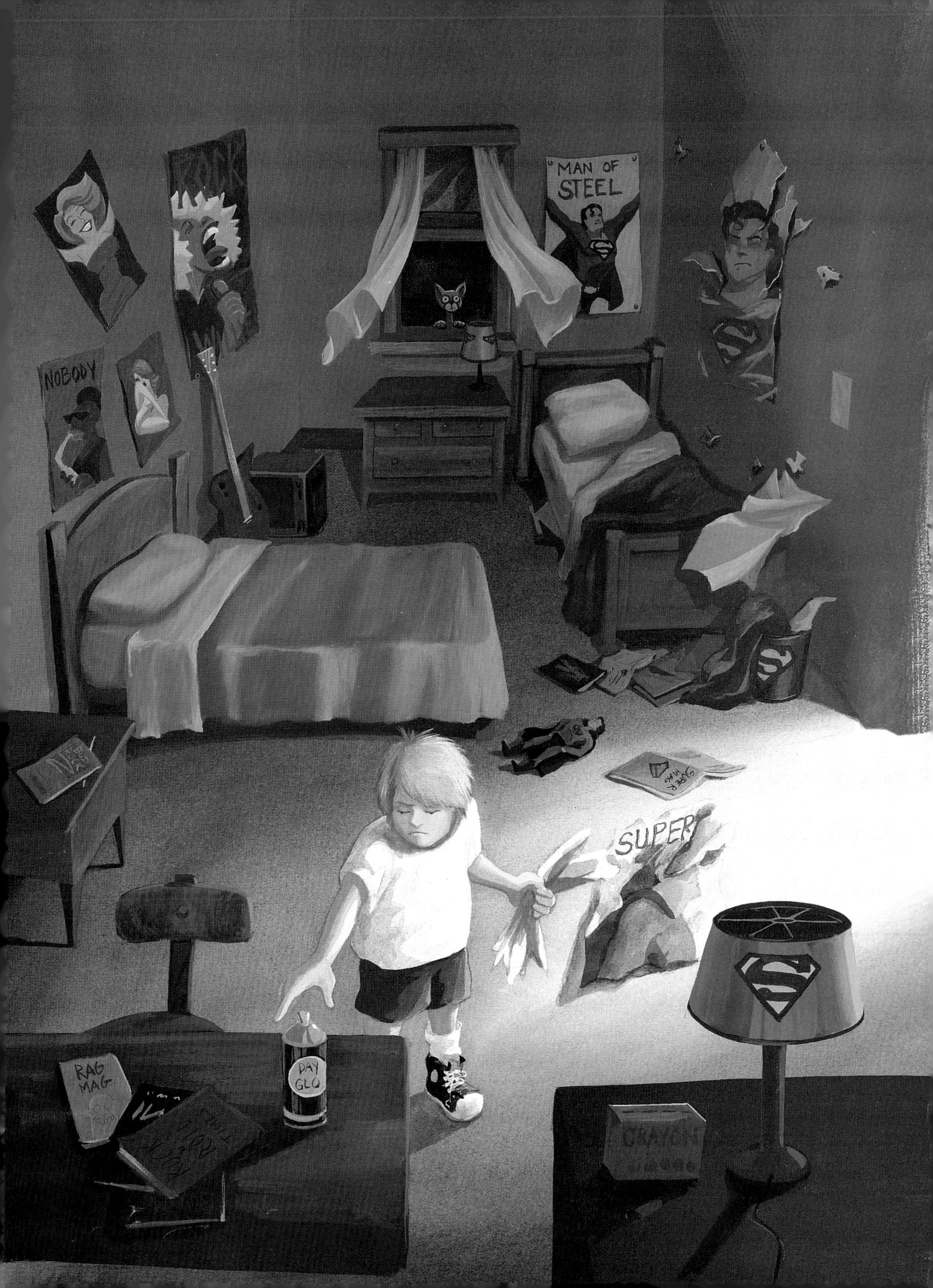
MAN OF STEEL
NOBODY
SUPER
DAY GLO
RAG MAG

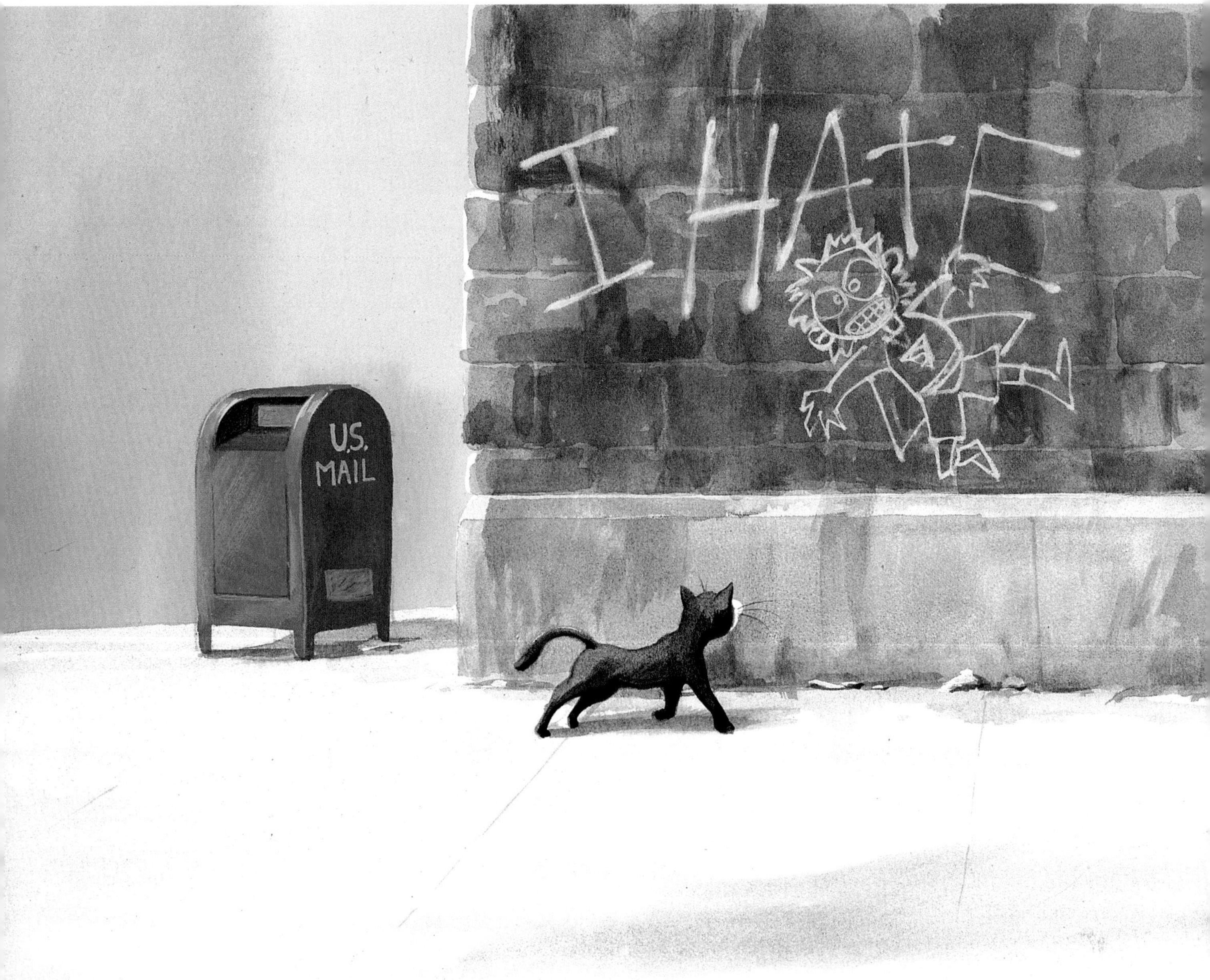
U.S.
MAIL
I HATE

The next day James sprayed the words "I HATE SUPERMAN!" in the alley beside his apartment building. He sprayed them on the walls of his school. Then he sprayed them on a street sign. He sprayed them all over the neighborhood, everywhere he could reach. "Why not foul up the

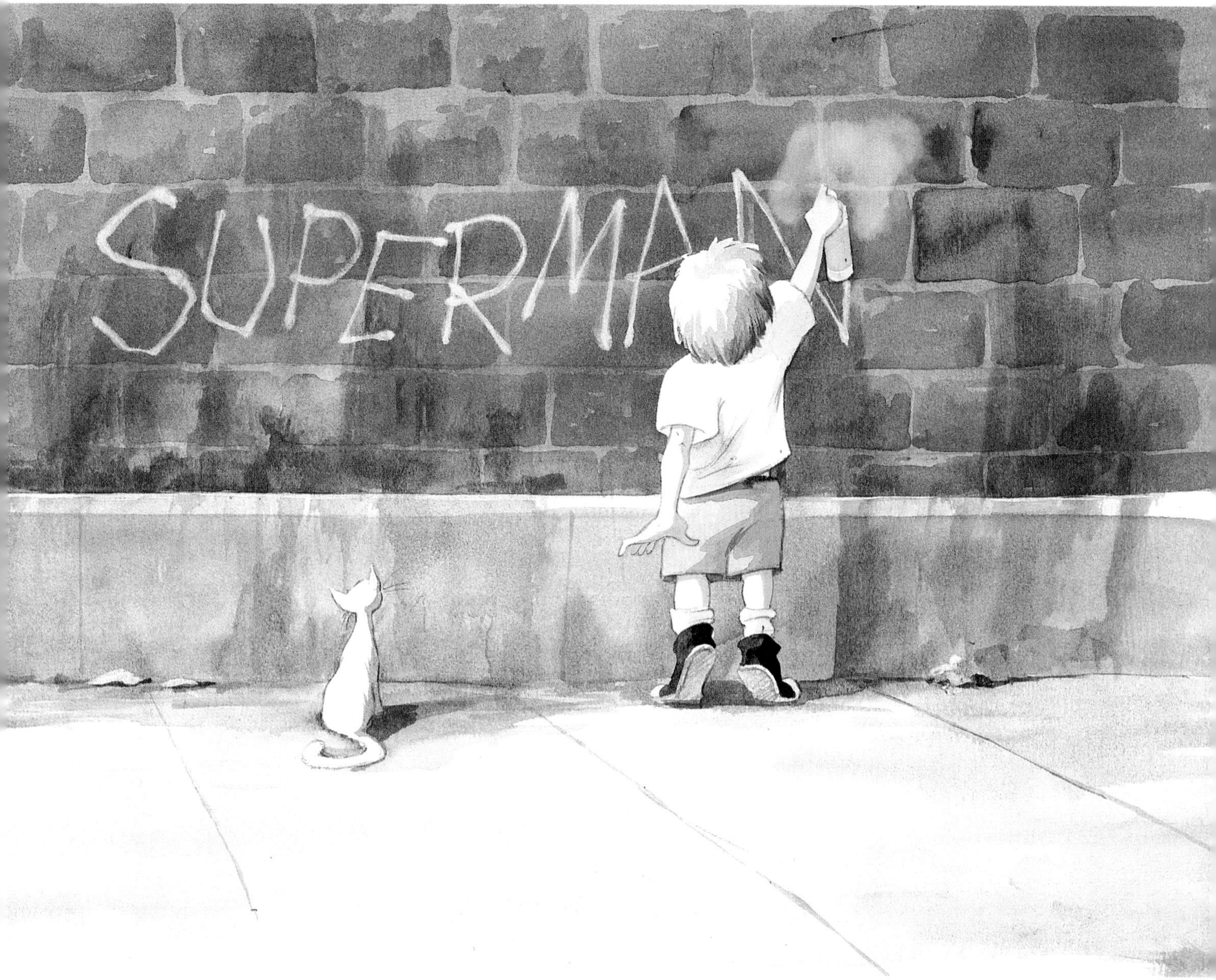
SUPERMAN

neighborhood," James muttered. "I tried to help Mr. Masire. I tried to be like Superman, and look where it got me!" He sprayed a big ugly snarl on Superman's face. "Superman could have let Mike go. But he sent him to jail. It's all his fault! I hate him!" James shouted. He didn't care who heard.

At the playground Mike's friend Richard sneered at James. "You're such a dweeb," he said. "You snitched on your own brother!"

James didn't even care that the boy was twice his size. He tackled Richard, forcing him to the ground. The boys rolled over and over until a passerby ran there to break up the fight.

"Are you crazy?" Richard yelled as James was pulled away, still kicking and screaming.

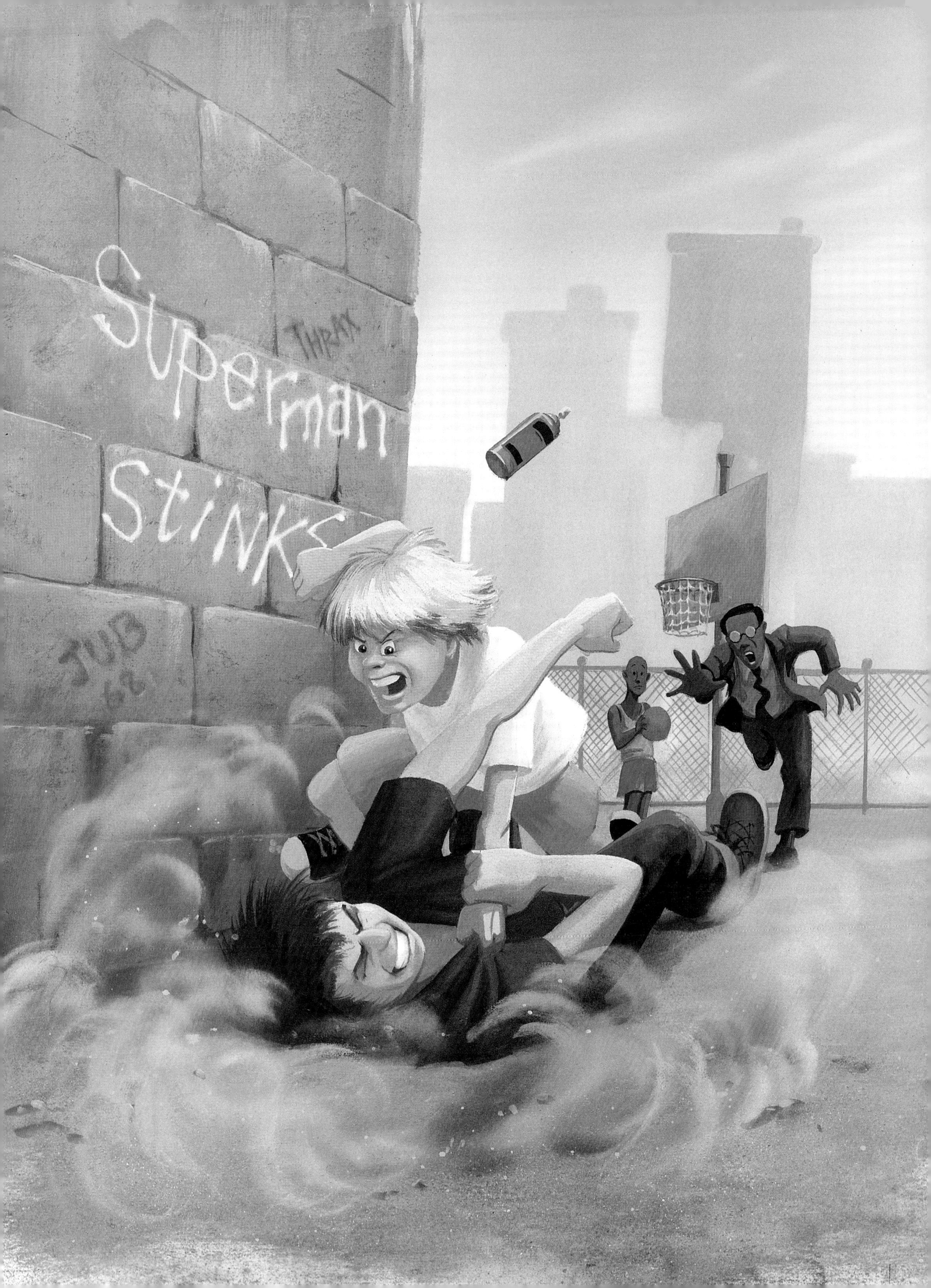
Superman
stinks
JUB

Later that day James crouched on the blacktop beneath the basketball hoop. The can of spray paint hissed out a Day-Glo "A," the second-to-last letter in Superman's name. *Superman flies over the city all the time! James thought. When he looks down, he'll see this! I can't wait! I want him to see it!*

James thought about his fight with Richard, and for the first time he hesitated. *Maybe Richard's right,* he thought. *Maybe I am crazy.*

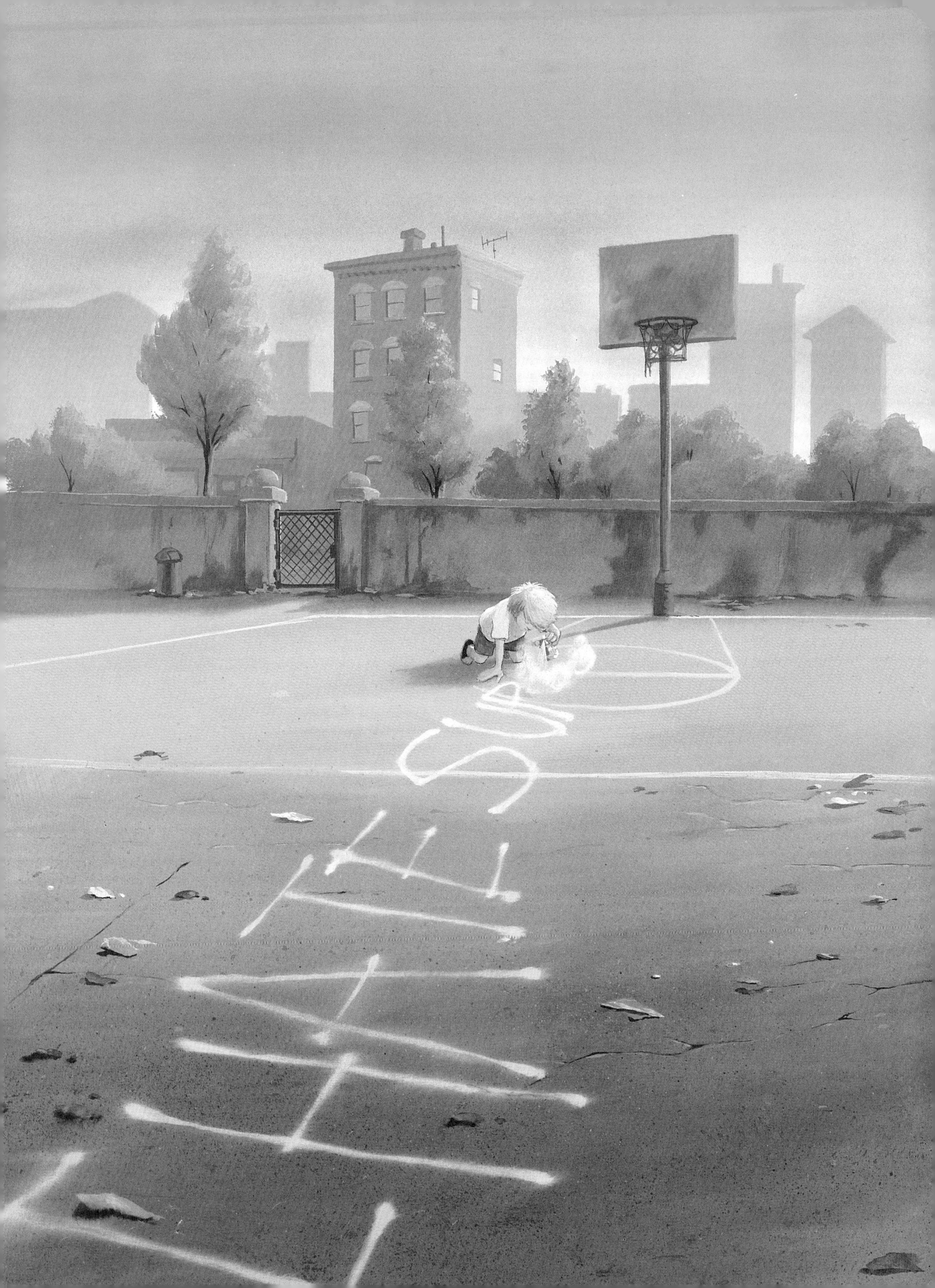

Just then James heard a thump on the blacktop behind him. He looked up, then turned away and kept on spraying. Even when the familiar shadow that fell over him moved closer, James refused to turn around again.

"It looks as if you're pretty mad at me!" Superman said.

"So you noticed!" James replied. When he finished, he read his words aloud. "I hate Superman!"

"It was hard not to notice," Superman said. "Your graffiti is all over the neighborhood."

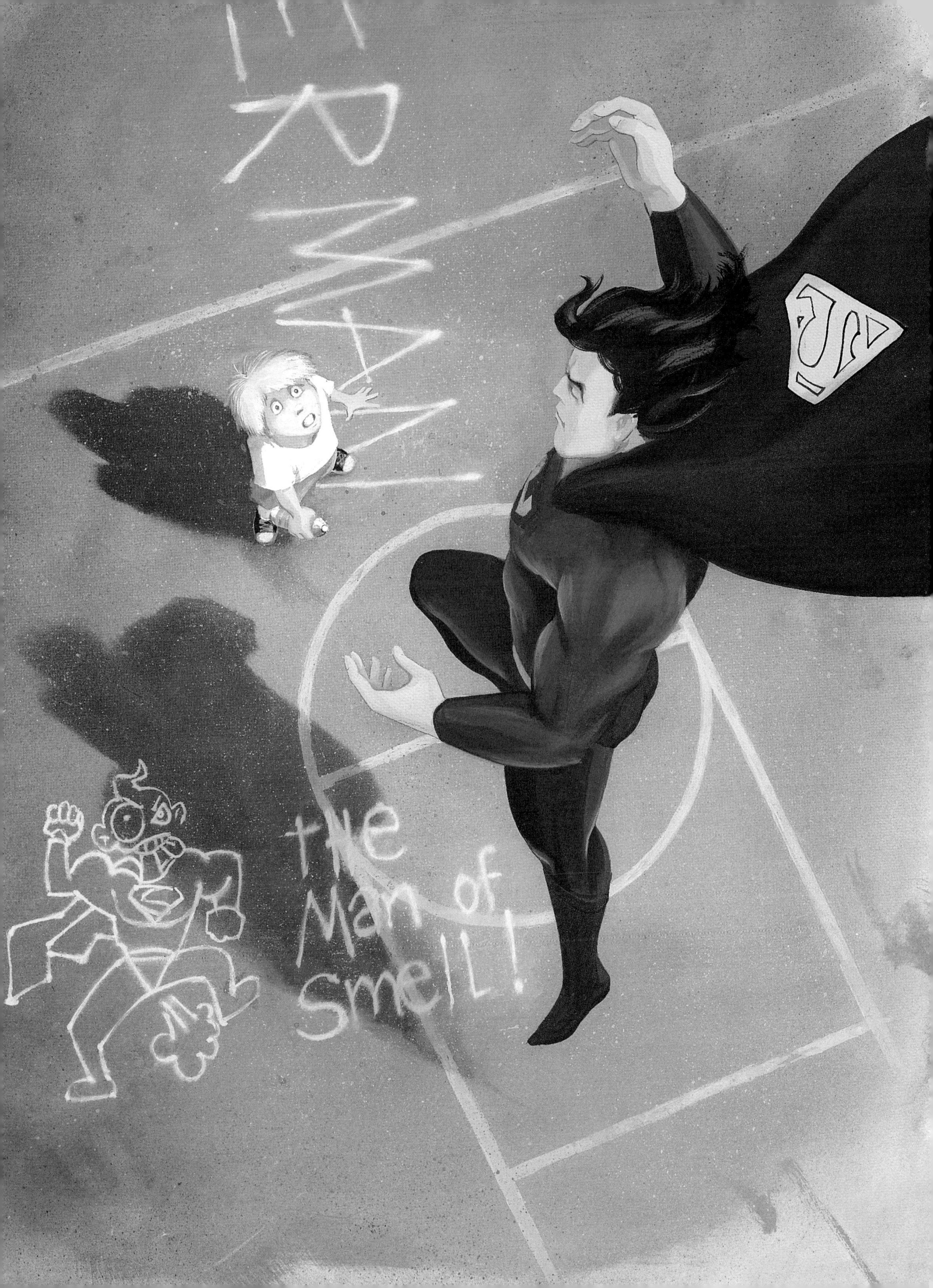
tHe Man of smelL!

"You think you know everything!" James shouted. He turned and threw the paint can at the Man of Steel. It hit him and bounced off his chest.

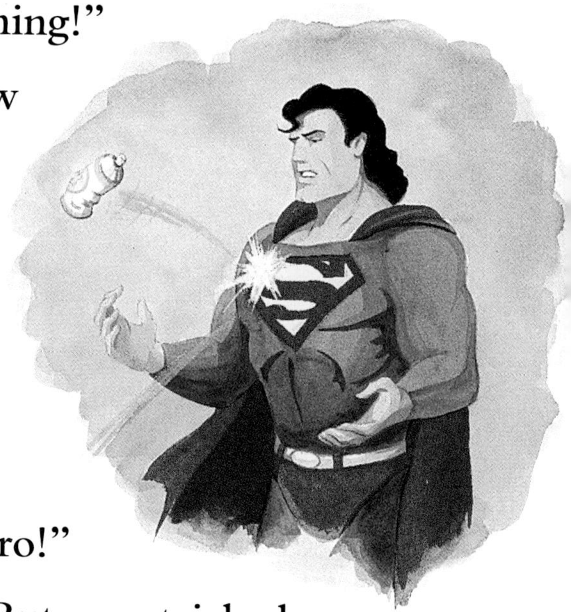

James plowed into Superman, pounding him as hard as he could with both fists.

"You pretend to be this big hero!" James cried. "And I believed you! But you tricked me! Now Mr. Masire thinks I'm a big hero, too! But I'm not! I'm a snitch! I don't want to be like you anymore!"

Superman let James hit him until the boy was just too tired to move. Then Superman gathered him into his arms and held him until James's sobs quieted.

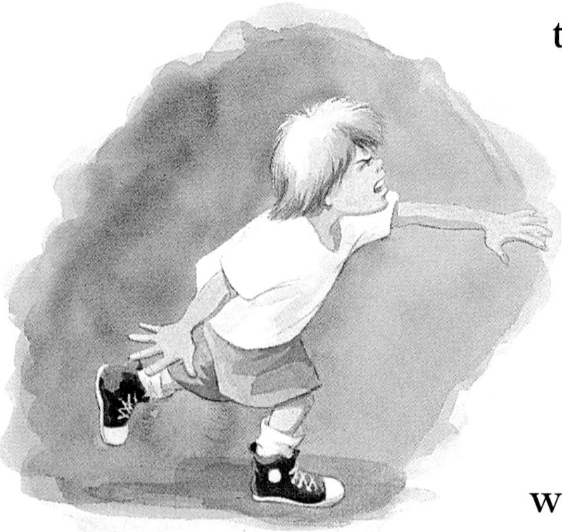

"I didn't arrest your brother because you betrayed him. I arrested him because what he was doing was wrong. There was a gun. People could have been seriously hurt," Superman said. "It's good to love your brother, but you don't have to act like him. Or me," Superman added.

The two stood in silence for a moment. Then Superman walked James home.

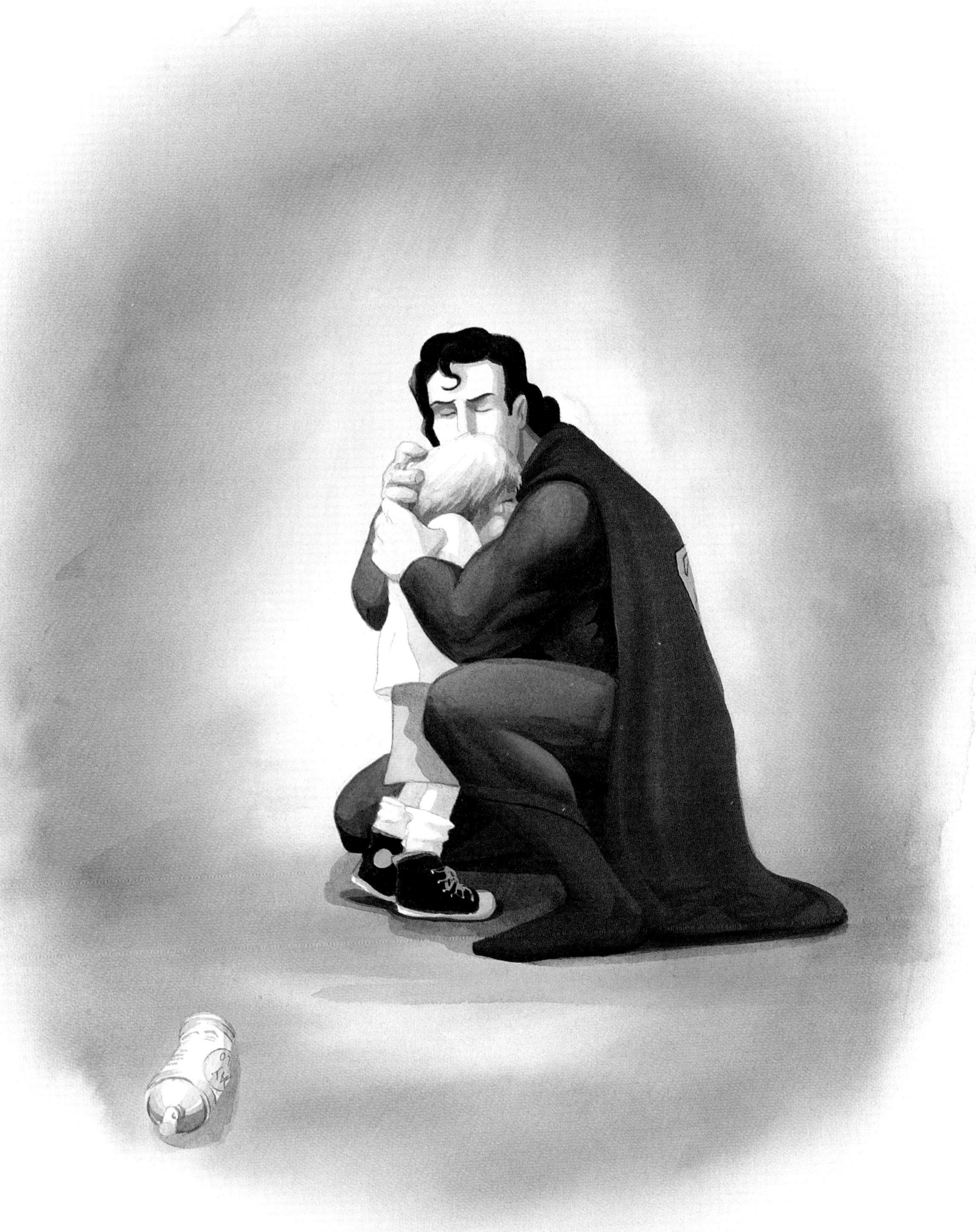

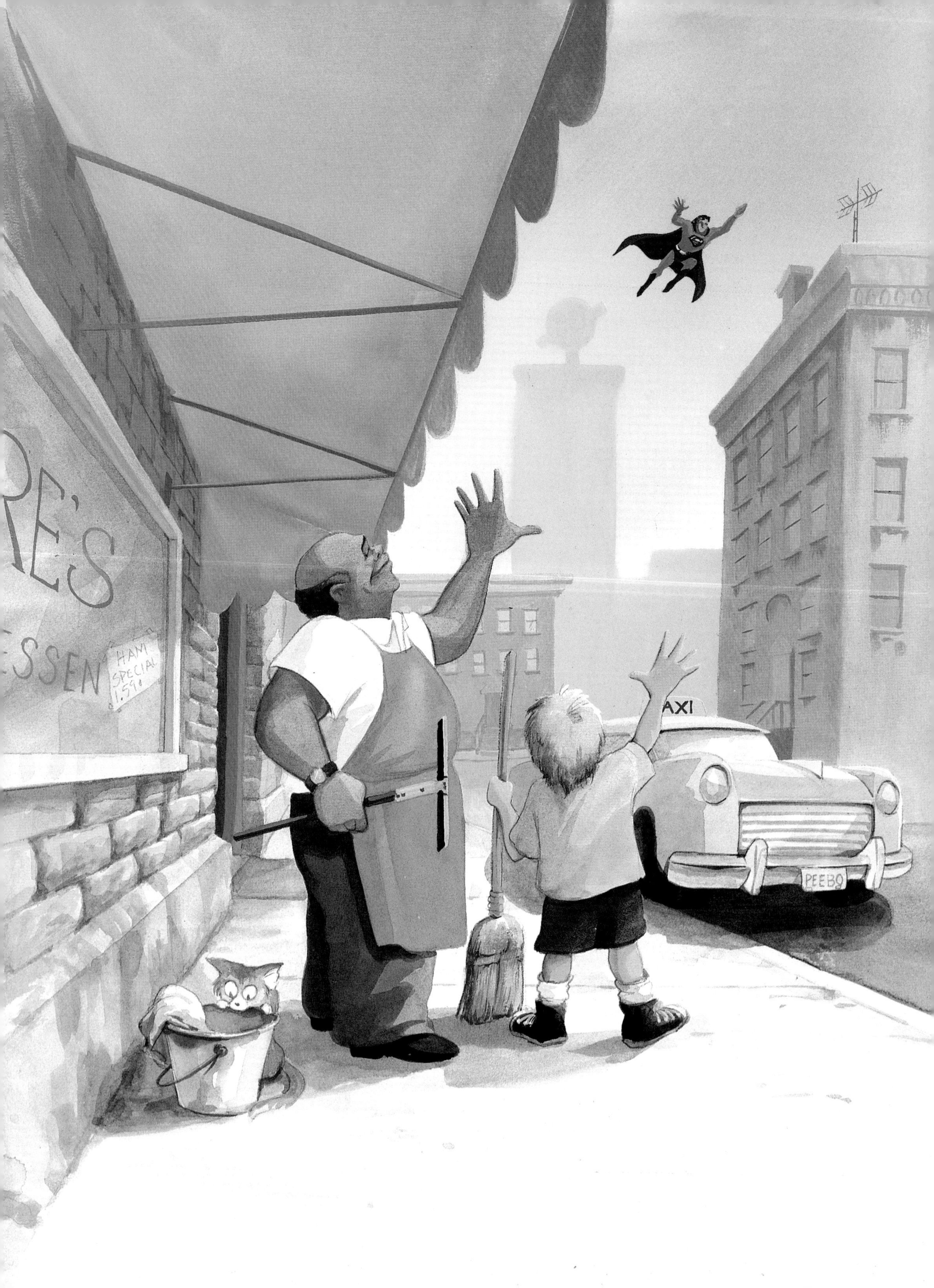
RE'S
ESSEN
HAM SPECIAL 1.59¢
AXI
PEEBO

The rest of that long, hot summer James stayed with Mr. Masire whenever his mother was at work. He let James drink all the sodas he wanted and even paid James for helping him. James and Mr. Masire still searched the sky for Superman. And most of the week James was happy.

Except on Saturdays.

On Saturdays he went with his mother to visit his brother in jail. James and his mother sat at a table on one side of a thick piece of plastic. Mike sat on the other side. They spoke to each other over a telephone.

"When you were arrested, you wouldn't look at me," James said to Mike one day. "I thought you hated me!"

"I didn't hate you!" Mike said to him sadly. "I was just ashamed. I knew I shouldn't have gone with my friends, but I did it anyway. I didn't want you to see me like that."

On Saturdays James spent a lot of time thinking about Mike and Superman and what had happened.

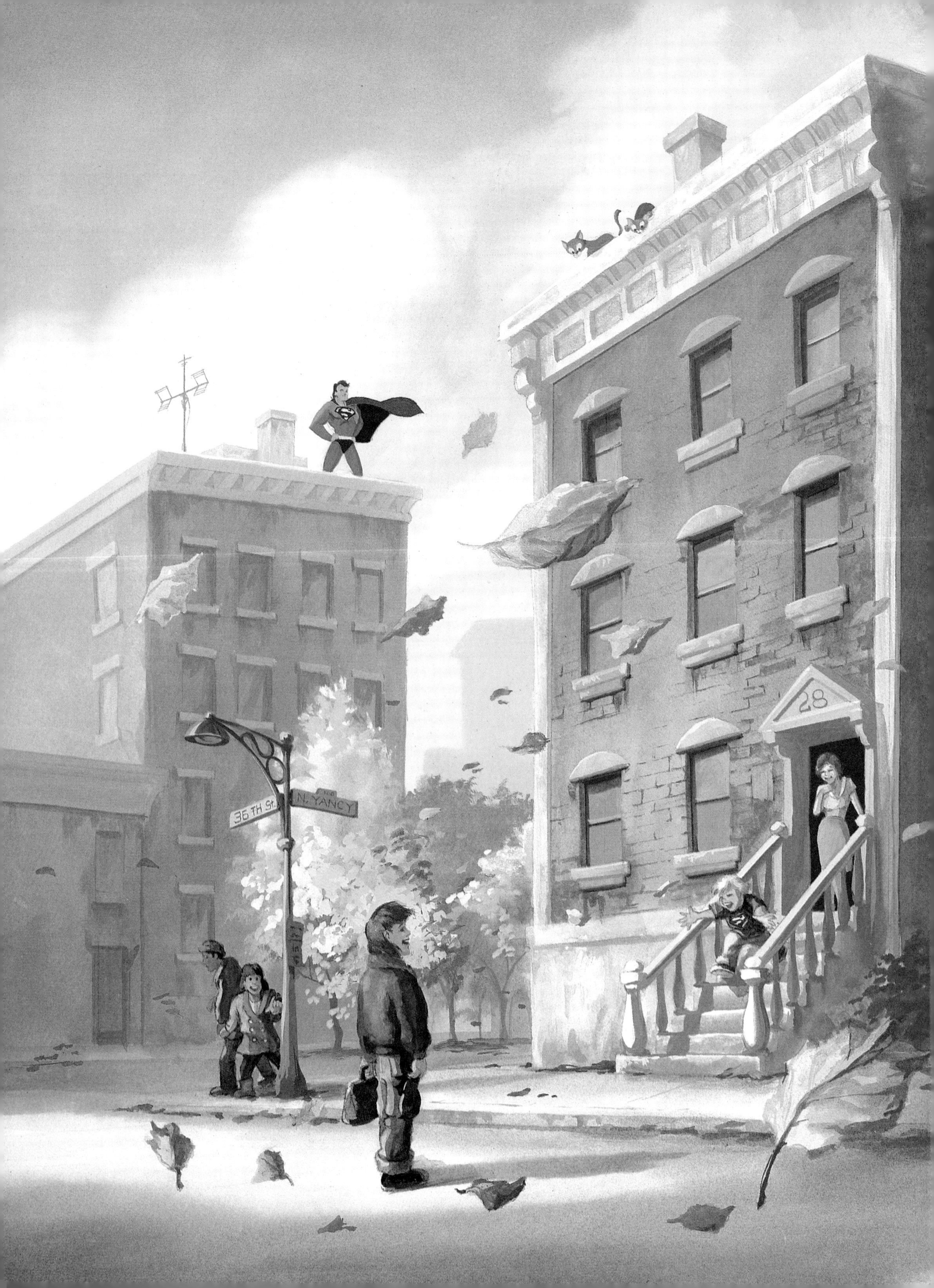
36TH St.
N. YANCY
28

At last Mike was released from jail.

"Mike! Mike! You're home!" James cried as he flung his arms around his brother. James's next words caught in his throat. "I'm sorry I got you arrested," he said for what felt like the hundredth time.

"Don't blame yourself," Mike said as he put his hands on his brother's shoulders. "I told you, it was my fault I got in trouble. It wasn't yours."

"That's what Superman says, too," James said as he hugged Mike close. "I love you, Mike. I'm glad you're my brother! I'm glad you're home."

I HATE SUPERMAN!

For Juli and Nikoli and especially Mike Carlin—L.S.

For Arthur Heinemann—K.A. & K.A.

Superman created by Jerry Siegel and Joe Shuster.

First Edition

Louise Simonson is the best-selling author of *Superman: Doomsday & Beyond*. She has written over a dozen comic book titles for both Marvel Comics and DC Comics, and is currently the writer of the comic book *Superman: Man of Steel*.

Kevin Altieri is the Emmy Award-nominated director of *Batman: The Animated Series*, and the upcoming *Gen^{13}*. His work for DC Comics includes covers for the popular *Superman & Batman Magazine*. He is also the writer and illustrator of the *Demon* comic, "Castle of the Damned." Kevin has been working in animation for over ten years.

Kathy Altieri is a former painter and supervisor at Disney Feature Animation where her credits included *The Lion King*, *Aladdin*, and *The Little Mermaid*, as well as a number of short cartoons and featurettes. She is currently the background supervisor and co-head of visual development for DreamWorks SKG. Kathy and her husband Kevin live with their three cats and three rats in Westchester, California.

ISBN 0-316-17806-3
Library of Congress Catalog Card Number 94-78023

10 9 8 7 6 5 4 3 2 1

WOR
Published simultaneously in Canada by Little, Brown & Company (Canada) Limited

Printed in the United States of America